Helen Stephens

Fleabag

Henry Holt and Company • New York

There was once a dog who had no name, and he had no home.

What he did have was **fleas**, but they weren't much company.

He lived all alone in the big city,

and he found his
dinner wherever
he could.

He liked to bark at the
huge blue things that
thundered past . . .

Woof!

Woof!

Woof!

. . . and to run in the big green place where he saw
lots of other dogs. The other dogs all had people to
take for walks. He wished he had a person, too.

Sometimes, he tried to join in the other dogs' games, but their people called him "fleabag" and told him to "shoo!"

Then one day he saw a boy with a ball, but no dog. The boy's big person was busy, and the boy had no one to play with. That didn't seem right.

So when the boy threw his ball,
the dog ran as fast as he could . . .

across the green stuff . . .

through the
pink things . . .

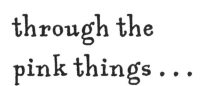

and caught it!

That was
fun. He had
never played
before.

The boy looked very
pleased. He tickled the
dog under the chin.
The dog liked that. He
had never been tickled before.

"Don't touch him, Bob!"
said the boy's big person.
"He's all dirty."

"I don't mind," said Bob. "I like him."

Over the next few days,
the dog looked out for his boy,

and the boy looked out for his dog.

The boy's big person
was usually too busy
to notice.

The boy and the dog
became great friends.

But then one day, the boy didn't feel
like playing. He was too sad.

He told the dog that his family were
moving the next day. They were going
far away, and he wouldn't be able to play
with the dog ever again.

The dog waggled his eyebrows as if
he understood, but he didn't really.

Then the boy's big person called out,
"Come on, Bob! Time to go home!
Leave that little fleabag alone now."

"I have to go with my mom," said the boy.
"I'll miss you." And he shook the dog's paw.

Then the boy followed his mom . . .
and the dog followed his boy . . .
all the way home.

That night, the boy couldn't sleep. When he looked out his window, he could see his dog sitting far below.

"I can't leave you behind," he thought—
and he decided to do something very scary.

He picked up his suitcase, which was already
packed for the move, stuffed a few cookies in his
pocket, and tiptoed out of the apartment.

He was scared as he
scampered down the stairs.

He was scared as the heavy
door shut behind him.

He was scared as he ran
to meet his friend.

"Come on, boy!" he said bravely.
"We're running away!"

The dog was very confused. What was his boy doing outside in the dark? He should be safe indoors with his big people. He sat very still.

"Come on!" said the boy. But the dog wouldn't move.

"Cookie?" said the boy. But the dog wouldn't budge.

"I'll just have to carry you," said the boy. But the dog wriggled free and tried to pull his boy back home.

Then he ran around and around him, barking.

Woof!

Woof!

Woof!

Woof!

Woof!

"Shush!" said the boy. "You'll wake up Mom and Dad!" That seemed like a good idea, so the dog went:

WOOF!

WOOF!

WOOF!

W

WOOF!

WOOF!

WOOF!

WOOF!

Woof!

Woof!

WOOF!

Woof!

WOOF!

OOF!

WOOOF!

WOOF!

WOOF!

...until a light
turned on, and a
worried face looked out.

The boy's big people seemed rather annoyed. They sent him straight back to bed.

Then one of them said, "I suppose this little fleabag can sleep here tonight."

"I think he deserves to," said the other. "He did look after Bob."

The dog was very excited. He had never slept in a real bed before.

The next day, the family took
everything out of their apartment and put it in an
enormous van. Then, when the van was full, they
got into their car. The dog was worried. Were his
people going somewhere without him?

Then the man said, "Come
on, little fleabag! Hop in!
You're coming with us."

And that's how the dog
with no name found a home!

The dog soon settled in.

Dad got rid of his fleas,
which was good.

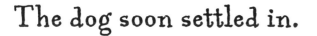

Mom got him nice and
clean, which wasn't so good.

Then Bob got him nice
and dirty all over again.

The dog listened while his family
tried to think of a name for him.

"Scruff?"
said Mom.

"Spike?"
said Dad.

"Ga-ga?"
said the baby.

But the only name that stuck was . . .

...Fleabag!

Fleabag was inspired by a
dog I met at Battersea Dogs
and Cats Home, a special place
for dogs who need new
homes. His name was
Fynn. He had lovely
bushy eyebrows and
seemed to enjoy being drawn. These are some
of the sketches I did. The day I met him he had
found a new home and was freshly shampooed
waiting for his new big people to collect him.
This book is dedicated to all the dogs at
Battersea Dogs and Cats Home.

Helen Stephens

Black ears

Black

Henry Holt and Company, LLC
Publishers since 1866
175 Fifth Avenue
New York, New York 10010
www.HenryHoltKids.com

Henry Holt® is a registered trademark of Henry Holt and Company, LLC.

First published in the United States in 2010 by Henry Holt and Company, LLC.
Distributed in Canada by H. B. Fenn and Company Ltd.
Originally published in the United Kingdom in 2008 by
Scholastic Children's Books (Alison Green Books).

Library of Congress Cataloging-in-Publication Data
Stephens, Helen.
Fleabag / Helen Stephens. — 1st American ed.
p.   cm.
Summary: A stray dog and a lonely boy become fast friends at a neighborhood park,
but everything changes when the boy's family decides to move away.
ISBN 978-0-8050-8975-2
[1. Dogs—Fiction. 2. Moving, Household—Fiction. 3. Dog adoption—Fiction.]
I. Title.
PZ7.S83213Fle 2010   [E]—dc22   2009009196

First American Edition—2010
Printed in August 2009 in Singapore by Tien Wah Press, Singapore,
on acid-free paper. ∞
10 9 8 7 6 5 4 3 2 1

Black fur
light Brown face &
legs & paws

Fynn Battersea Dogs Home 21/4/06